Possum Magic

Written by Mem Fox   Illustrated by Julie Vivas

An Omnibus Book from Scholastic Australia

For Chloë, Ana and Kate

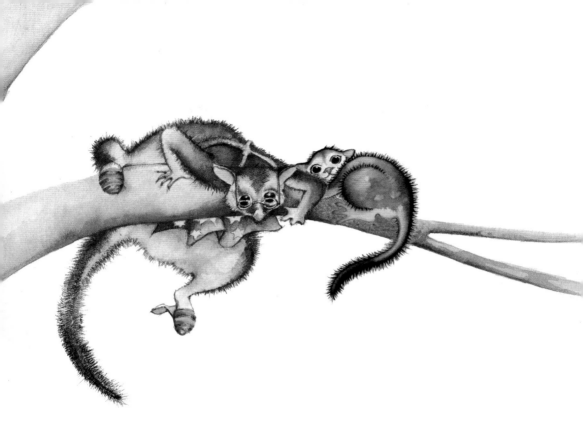

Once upon a time, but not very long ago,
deep in the Australian bush lived two possums.
Their names were Hush and Grandma Poss.

Grandma Poss made bush magic.
She made wombats blue and
kookaburras pink.

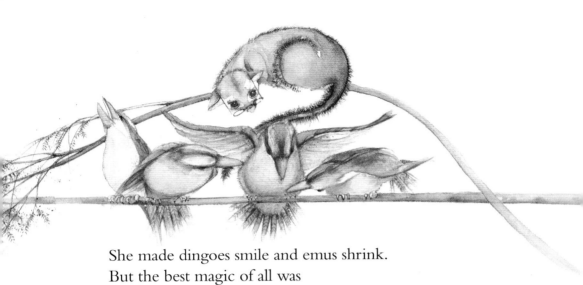

She made dingoes smile and emus shrink.
But the best magic of all was

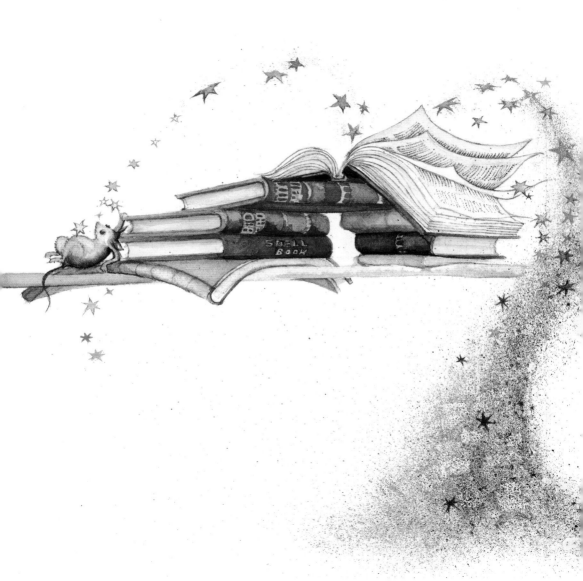

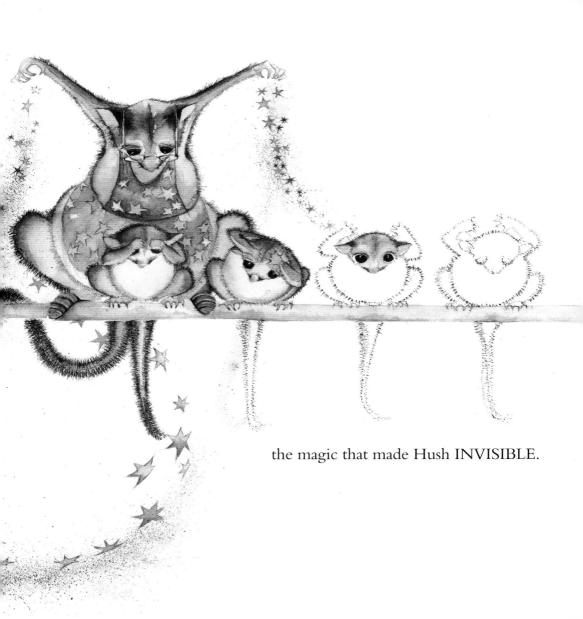

the magic that made Hush INVISIBLE.

What adventures Hush had!
Because she couldn't be seen
she could be squashed by koalas.

Because she couldn't be seen she could slide down kangaroos.

Because she couldn't be seen she was safe from snakes,
which is why Grandma Poss had made her invisible
in the first place.

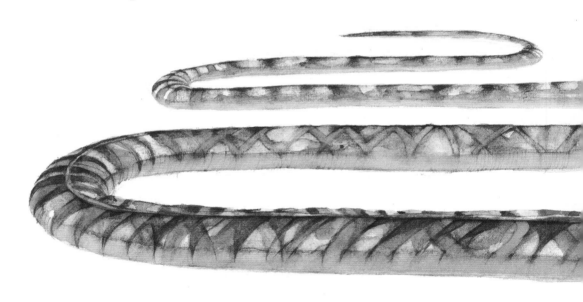

But one day, quite unexpectedly, Hush said,
"Grandma, I want to know what I look like.
Please could you make me visible again?"

"Of course I can," said Grandma Poss,
and she began to look through her magic books.

She looked into this book
and she looked into that.
There was magic for thin
and magic for fat,
and magic for tall
and magic for small,
but the magic she was looking for
wasn't there at all.

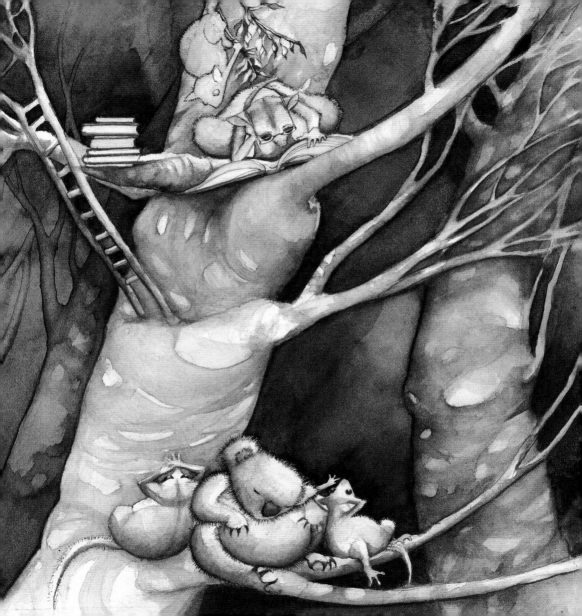

Grandma Poss looked miserable.

"Don't worry, Grandma," said Hush.
"I don't mind."

But in her heart of hearts she did.

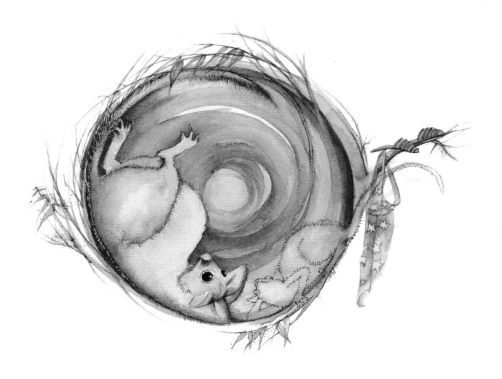

All night long Grandma Poss thought and thought.

The next morning, just before breakfast,
she shouted, "It's something to do with food!
People food – not possum food. But I can't remember what.
We'll just have to try and find it."

So later that day,
they left the bush where they'd always been
to find what it was that would make Hush seen.

They ate Anzac biscuits in Adelaide,
mornay and Minties in Melbourne,
steak and salad in Sydney
and pumpkin scones in Brisbane.

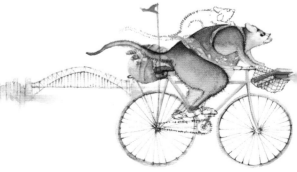

Hush remained invisible.

"Don't lose heart!" said Grandma Poss.
"Let's see what we can find in Darwin."

It was there, in the far north of Australia,
that they found a Vegemite sandwich.

Grandma Poss crossed her claws and crossed her feet.

Hush breathed deeply and began to eat.

"A tail! A tail!" shouted both possums at once.
For there it was. A brand new, visible tail!

Later, on a beach in Perth, they ate a piece of pavlova.
Hush's legs appeared. So did her body.

"You look wonderful, you precious possum!" said Grandma Poss.
"Next stop – Tasmania."

And over the sea they went.

In Hobart, late one night, in the kitchens
of the casino, they saw a lamington on a plate.
Hush closed her eyes and nibbled.

Grandma Poss held her breath – and waited.
"It's worked! It's worked!" she cried.

And she was right. Hush could be seen from head to tail.
Grandma Poss hugged Hush, and they both danced
"Here We Go Round the Lamington Plate" till early in the morning.

From that time onwards, Hush was visible.
But once a year, on her birthday,
she and Grandma Poss ate a Vegemite sandwich,
a piece of pavlova and half a lamington,
just to make sure that Hush stayed visible forever.

And she did.

Omnibus Books
175–177 Young Street, Parkside SA 5063
an imprint of Scholastic Australia Pty Ltd (ABN 11 000 614 577)
PO Box 579, Gosford NSW 2250.
www.scholastic.com.au

Part of the Scholastic Group
Sydney · Auckland · New York · Toronto · London · Mexico City · New Delhi ·
Hong Kong · Buenos Aires · Puerto Rico

First published in 1983.
First published in revised edition in 2004.
Reprinted in 2004 (three times), 2005 (twice), 2006, 2007 (twice),
2008 (twice), 2009, 2010 (twice), 2011, 2012.
First published in this edition in 2013.
Reprinted in 2013, 2014 (twice), 2015.
Text copyright © Mem Fox, 1983.
Illustrations copyright © Julie Vivas, 1983.

National Library of Australia Cataloguing-in-Publication entry
Fox, Mem.
Possum magic.
30th anniversary mini ed.
For pre-school age.
ISBN 978 1 74299 005 7 (hbk.)
1. Pseudocheiridae – Juvenile fiction. 2. Magic – Juvenile fiction. I. Vivas, Julie. II. Title.
A823.3

Julie Vivas used watercolour for the illustrations in this book.
Typeset in Bembo by Clinton Ellicott, Adelaide.
Printed by RR Donnelley, China.